HAPPY STORIES

MY DEAR DEER FRIEND

TALL THIN MAN

A SHORT STORY

MY MYNA BIRD WITH A MIND

A MAGIC MOMENT

DOG VS CAT

William Milborn

authorHOUSE®

AuthorHouse™
1663 Liberty Drive
Bloomington, IN 47403
www.authorhouse.com
Phone: 1 (800) 839-8640

Published by AuthorHouse 05/29/2019

ISBN: 978-1-7283-1412-9 (sc)
ISBN: 978-1-7283-1411-2 (e)

Print information available on the last page.

This book is printed on acid-free paper.

MY DEAR DEER FRIEND

BY

WILLIAM L. MILBORN

MY DEAR DEER FRIEND

I am known hereabouts as Billy Boy but my friends call me "Lover Boy". My good friend who works with me at the mill is called Bobby Boy. We go in there everyday clean as could be–clean uniforms, everything–but when we leave, we are as white as ghosts. We cannot keep that flour or whatever else we are milling from coating us.

Today, we left at the end of the second shift and didn't bother to change or wash our white faces or white hair. We looked like two ghosts leaving the job that night. I did grab my coat that I wear because it had my wallet in it. We are going to stop at our favorite little place that we like to go after work. As they say, "whetting one's whistle" can be the best part of the day.

Into Bobby Boy's truck we went and away we went to Tobey's Bar and Grill. It was more of a bar than a grill. We made short time in getting out of that truck and into the bar seat which had freed up and where many of the first shift boys had already done their drinking and were staggering out of that place bound for home or apartments. As we entered this watering hole, friends would slap us on the back just to see the mill flour explode from our uniforms and to see the mill flour cloud the air around us with whiteness. A lot of the guys lived alone for some reason. We always said that our high school is too short on girls. The rich ones went off to college and somewhere the others were pressed into marrying by an unfortunate incident that occurred on prom night and other nights as well. But that is not my story.

Bobby Boy and I were introduced to some new beer drink that night. It was Bobby Boy that got me drinking this thing called "Boiled Beer".

It wasn't long before the smoke and the music, and the drinks were causing everybody to laugh and sing and tell naughty stories. That's when—you know—we are under the right circumstances to leave.

I guess my friend Bobby Boy had too many drinks. He was not in the men's room and sure enough had left, and he left me without a way to get home. I had no car. I guess he thought I must have driven too.

I said, "Bar Keep, I will have one more of those boiled drinks. It's my 'one-for-the-road' before I leave." Thank goodness my home was only two miles on down the road from this old "watering hole".

I whistled and sang for awhile as I walked home and then I suddenly became horribly sleepy and a bit weak. I hoped I could get home before I fell out from those drinks. I thought I must be one-half of the way home by now so I decided to squat and rest a bit. Even though this was a fine road it was seldom used. It was still considered a country road. A poor town's roads will be of dirt and gravel. I cared that they were paved because they were warm and each night would become cooler. I just sat on that warm pavement. I felt pretty good. I'll just lay close to the side of this unused road. I will stay warm and nap a spell. My wife won't know because she is visiting her folks in Carthage.

I don't know how long I rested and napped. I saw a car swerving by and heard tires squeal and then I saw the lights flash on and off towards the side of the road. I heard a bump and within several seconds I felt a body, I guess, bump right into the side of me. I was just too numb to move and it was too hard to see in the darkness. I was practically in a coma from that beer boil that I had. So that body that was next to me felt like a part of the body which was throw over my legs while the upper part laid very close to me. As far as I know no other traffic came by.

I woke up thinking that I had only slept an hour. I felt pretty good and opened my eyes and I was nose-to-nose with some large, beautiful eyes. They were staring directly into mine. We both gave a sudden jerk in surprise because those very large eyes were looking at me so that I could see my own reflection. It was a deer. A fairly small deer but I could hardly tell until I could stand up. That wild deer was petrified. I saw that its hip was bloody but that is all. I pulled myself out from underneath the deer, rubbing behind its ears all the time. I just kept rubbing its ears. It thrust its body forwards and this little doe stood favoring his rear left leg. I felt its leg. The deer didn't move. Its leg wasn't broken. I guess it was too much in fear, but it must have been in considerable pain or stupor because of its right hip. I pet the deer and continued putting my hand behind its ears—one at a time—rubbing and scratching. It knew somehow, I could be trusted.

I would walk that deer home with me and call a veterinarian to fix it up. No problem. That deer hugged my right side every step of the way. There were a few cars now. There were guys going to work and everyone was sticking their heads out of their cars and wondering what kind of a big dog that was. What else could it be? It wasn't a horse or a cow, sheep or goat. It had to be a dog. What else could it be? No one would guess it was a wild deer.

We walked along side of the highway and finally pushed the fence gate open and we climbed a few steps to the porch and I took my key from under the mat and opened the door. The deer walked in first and laid down in the middle of the floor. I took a cushion and propped it under its head thinking it might want to rest and it did.

The phone rang. It was Bobby. He said, "You left your coat in my car." I said, "Well, you left me without a ride home!" Bobby said, "It must have been the 'boiler maker' because I forgot that I left you." I said, "Is that what it is called?" Bobby said, "It is whiskey poured into a beer or visa versa." I said, "Well Bobby, I couldn't make it home." He said, "Did you meet somebody?" I said, "Yes I had a meeting just as I left the bar and started to walk home." Bobby said, "Oh, you did? It wasn't one of those hostess kind of girls was it?" I said, "She was a deer!" Bobby said, "I'm sure. She had to have been, 'Lover Boy'." I said, "NO! NO! NO! A doe!" Bobby said, "Yes, 'Lover Boy', those girls do want dough, don't they?" I said "She was a lovely deer. It wasn't my fault, just hurt." I added, "I took her home with me." He said, "You didn't! Did you hurt her feelings?" I said, "No, and she is with me right now Bobby Boy! Now Bobby, I will need my dough!" Bobby said, "Yes, I see that you need your dough." I said, "Now bring it to me right now Bobby Boy. I'll be here. I'm going to give her some milk and I'll have coffee." He said, "She drinks milk?" I said, "Yes, Bobby Boy. We are just laying here on the floor. We are tired from the walk and I'm still trying to recover from this hang over." He said, "What if your sweet wife comes in? What will you do and say? You have to tell her!" I said, "I will tell her and she won't care." Bobby said, "Oh yes she will 'Lover Boy'!"

No sooner than I had hung up from Bobby, I called the veterinarian's office and said, "I may have a broken leg for you to take care of." He said, "One of your critters standing in the street again?" He was speaking of my lazy old hound dog who happens to be laying on the couch taking it all in. You'd think my hound would bawl or come over and check us out, but no, he just laid there. What was he thinking? I said, "Well, something like that doctor. See you soon." Thirty minutes later the vet came and rapped on the door. I said, "Come in. Deer is in here." He said, "Don't call me dear."

I said, "A deer with a broken leg is in here." The vet looked and sure enough, when he saw the deer he said, "Oh no, I don't think so. I have treated deer plenty of times. They get up on their back feet and box at me!" I said, "No, this is a very friendly doe." I added, "See how I scratch it behind its ear? I give it milk and bring it cereal to eat. I gave it breakfast today."

The vet came close to my deer and felt its legs and said, "No Break! Just sore and sprained. The hip is very badly bruised and probably sore. I brought you a vial of pain pills and you may give them to your friend. Have a nice day."

I drove my old truck to the country store and bought every box of cereal they had, corn, wheat, oats and barley. The check out counter manager said, "Is this some kind of fad diet you are going on Billy Boy?" I said, "I guess so. You don't have to worry about that out-of-date cereal you have on your shelves." I took it all. I drove home and stored those boxes of cereal in every open space that our shelves had to offer.

The next day Doe Deer and I (I now called her Doe Deer) walked to the front yard. I put a rope around her beck so she wouldn't stray and could enjoy the grasses. Before long there was a parade of cars and the passersby would stare out of their windows at this "big dog" I had on a rope. They would drive up close to the fence and ask what kind of a "dog" it was. Some would ask, "Is that a deer?" I said, "It's a doe deer. It just happens to be a dear friend of mine."

Soon there was a line of people along the sidewalk next to the fence waiting their turn to pet my Doe Deer. They said, "It's so friendly. Can we pet it?" I walked my Doe Deer to the fence and the young lady and the little girl reached through the fence to pet my friend. I said, "Everyone, this is my dear friend. I think Doe Deer has to go to the pasture and do her business." Away we went to the pasture. I removed the rope thinking that when I did, I would probably never see my dear friend again. Even with her injured leg, Doe Deer bounced off in a three-legged hop through the tall grasses. I sat on a stump and watched. You could see the tall grasses moving where ever the deer was exploring. In minutes here came that three-legged little deer trotting back to me. In her mouth she had an ear of corn which she left on my lap. I wanted to think that she brought it just for me, but, in truth, she wanted me to feed it to her. I couldn't help myself. I cried. This deer loved me. How lonely am I? My wife will probably ultimately enjoy a deer at the table for breakfast, lunch and dinner because she was so friendly.

I sat for the longest time on that stump holding that ear of corn and scratching that deer's ear. We went into the house through the back entrance. Doe Deer thought I should go in the front and I had to convince Doe Deer this was the same house. She strolled in and went to where my chair was. She sat near my chair and laid her head right on the place where I would sit.

Right then I found a way to use that word I heard on T.V. The word was epiphany. I knew right then I wanted to take Doe Deer to petting zoos, store openings and other events. We would earn our keep in this fashion. I would give notice to my Mill Manager. I knew Doe Deer would be popular and a hit wherever she went and cause us to get more bookings.

It was the next day when my wife Joanne returned home. My wife, as I expected, had some real mixed emotions. It took nearly a week before she decided she loved Doe Deer as much as I.

I said, "We are going to have some fun. You and I will be paid to take part in petting zoo activities. We will be paid by companies and businesses to take Doe Deer to their stores for the kids to pet. Doe Deer won't get bored and probably eat too much. We will have the fun of travel and make a living at the same time. I dread the day when Doe Deer would become too old and she would have to give up her 'acting' career and retire. You know we can always stop doing this and can have our dough and then we can come home and back to doing something else. Doe Deer will have changed our lives. In closure what really changed my life was the drinking of the many 'Boiler Makers' on the nights I had free from work."

THE TALL THIN MAN

BY

WILLIAM L. MILBORN

THE TALL THIN MAN

I am so consumed by the character that I have written about in a previous book that I now feel a real need to tell you about this man called Booker T. T. Masters.

The tall, thin man reached seven feet in height. He has long black hair with a smile that was captivating to all the he spoke to. He was, in all ways, a human superman that I wish to tell you about.

Even during his formative years, from the day he could walk, his family and friends would say, "How could he do that?" He was walking by the age of one and making conversation by the age of two. He could grasp the words and the meanings of all things said to him in person and on the T.V. Booker's mind could process that information and somehow had the power to respond intelligently to questions asked of him. He would even ask questions of the people about the thoughts and visions of the current day! At the age of six!

Teachers knew not how to evaluate Booker and did not know what grade in school he should be placed. Second grade–at five feet tall? His teachers thought "How can he fit in?" The other students shied away from him and began calling him a freak and stupid. That is what kids do when they can't understand and have a fear of someone looking so different from them.

Soon there were spelling bees and our tall thin boy never failed to outscore everyone in the bee, even though the spelling challenge was for all, up to and including the eighth grade.

In spite of Booker's intelligence, he could not quite fathom the way he was treated and how people looked upon him. Through grade school and most of mid-school, psychiatrists were now giving poor Booker, our tall, thin boy, every mental test they knew how to give.

They said, "Booker, you know you are not normal and the tests revealed the highest scores ever achieved in their testing." Now, when their scholastic geniuses came together, they agreed that since they did not know how to evaluate him, they would need to have the teachers pass him on to a higher grade. Now, our tall, thin boy, was nearly six feet and much taller than the other students and his teachers.

Booker somehow knew algebra, trigonometry and higher math. He knew all the countries of the world and oceans and rivers of the world too. The teachers said, "How?" Booker said, "I just listen and read a lot of books!" They then asked, "Well, how do you come to so many conclusions about politicians and people?" Booker said, "That's easy! I just listen and look at them and theorize as to what their intent might be."

Our tall, thin boy is now six feet and is in high school. The principal asked, "What year should we put this young boy in at the age of twelve?" More meetings had been held regarding the tall, thin boy than anyone could recollect.

The sophomore sports coach said, "Well, the young lad is certainly smart, but let's see how well he could do in sports. He can't be strong at his age and he must be awkward, so let's start him out at something easy to see if his physical skills can match his mental abilities." Booker stated, "No, I am no one's puppet and I am not sure I even like sports because someone's got to lose!" The coach said, "That's true Booker, there are always winners and losers. So far you have been nothing but a winner! I'll wait Booker, you wonderful tall, thin/ boy, until you are thirteen. So, spend your twelfth year as you please."

Booker said, "I thank you Sir!" The high school staff said, "Well, what do you offer Booker to try to win now? The Senior math teach said, "Give him a shot at chess!" They did, and of course, he achieved a skill level where he could challenge chess players at a national level. It seemed like that all the teachers could say was, "How could he do that? How could he do that?" That year of constant chess tournaments determined just how intuitive our tall, thin boy was.

Finally, Booker's thirteenth year came around and he was looking at playing sports in his junior and senior years of high school. He did not think he was capable of going against all the other students in all sports and activities. Indeed, he did find himself a bit awkward. So, Booker decided to take dance classes to adjust his body to poise and control. Oh my, Booker took as his first class, Ballet. Even the sports coaches did not want to talk to him now. Booker's teacher taught him all the elementary moves and Booker thought, "Thank God there are two boys in the class!" Soon Booker was exercising at the bar with the girls to the many steps and positions that a ballerina must learn. In fact, in a few months Booker had learned to control his long, tall, big six-foot two-inch frame in doing these pirouettes and plies, one after another, after another. The girl ballerinas stopped and stood at the bar just ogling this tall, six foot two-inch thirteen-year old doing the dance steps and jumping that only the most skilled make professional ballet men could do on stage. The teacher, herself highly skilled, had to grab the protective bar to steady herself in witnessing a miracle of the tall, thin boy performing the most exacting dances of all in ballet.

Now Booker is fourteen and a junior in high school. Sports coaches no longer ignored our tall, thin boy and chose to try him out at various sports.

The basketball coach especially had an eye on Booker because of his height. That first day at basketball practice, there was consistent running and dribbling and passing the ball but no shooting. After practice, the coach said, "Hit the showers!"

He did and found himself being ridiculed by the guys who saw that he was totally hairless. They said, "Look at that fool with the foot-long hotdog with nothing but hair on his head!" It was only because of his six-foot, five- inch frame that they hesitated in pursuing their teasing. In fact, they told him "Booker, you pass the ball really good and you are fast on the court and dribble really good too!" The coach stuck his head in the shower and said, "Good job, Booker!" That surprised everyone.

Another day has come for Booker on the court. This time they concentrated on shooting skills. It is then that he discovered something he had that is paramount to the rest of the story. The best way to say it is that I some way he was in tune with nature. In feeling the weight of the ball and judging the distance to the hoop, his mind adjusted to the speed in which he could toss the ball.

He could feel the finger's pressure that he should put on that ball so he could achieve that arc to the center of the basketball hoop. Booker stood at the three- point line and placed one basketball after another into the center of that hoop without a miss. Other team members said, "No—can't be! It's a trick!" Some even said, "It's a miracle! We will never lose again!" Every other player attempted to do the same.

All of us then practiced the passing game running figure eights, back and forth from one end of the basketball court to the other.

There was a planned passing game at the opponent's end of the court and they practiced that too, even though they knew that might no longer be necessary if all they had to do was pass it to Booker. Even students not involved in their own games were coming to the bleachers just to sit and watch the practice sessions.

It was a different day now when the coach said, "Hit the showers." Booker was treated like the man of the hour even though there was much jealousy.

They quietly said to Booker, "Pass it to me now and then and let us put in in and score points!" Some of them reminded him, "We have a reputation with the girls and like to appear as winners too." Booker said, "Okay! Will do!"

Booker dropped out of basketball early per the coach's request so he could play football. The coach looked at me and said, "Can you do anything on the football field?" Booker said, "I don't know coach!" The coach said, "We are going to find out!!"

It was a chilly fall day when football practice began. The coach said, my six-foot, six-inch tall man, what do you think you can do for us on the field of sweet dreams and sweat?" The coach asked, "Can you run?" Booker said, "Yes Sir!" He said, "How fast?" Booker said, "Don't know Sir!" The coach said, "I will put you to the test today. I will be at the end of the fifty-yard dash line and you will start at the other end of this fifty-yard dash line and when you hear the gun go off, you run like the devil himself is chasing you." Booker said, "Yes Sir!"

Booker took his spot. He heard the gun and ran like the wind. He was timed at 4.5 seconds. The coach said, "Let me see that clock!" And like all people he said, "How did you do that?" Booker said, "With much effort coach!" Others tried out for this sport. Of course, no one could touch his score time. One other could run at 5.1 seconds. The coach said, "Okay, I'm going to introduce you to this ball. It is called a football!" Booker said, "I know! I know!" The coach asked, "Do you think, if you are running down the field, you could catch the ball while running?" Booker said, "Easy, Sir!" Booker also said, "With the size of my hands I think I can—not sure—but I think I can!"

That would be Booker's position on the high school football team. They won every game they played except one. That was because Booker got the mumps on the last game of the season. They lost the last regional game because they had no Booker. Our Booker, the tall, thin man, was so ashamed.

Booker is now in his senior year and is as tall as he will be at seven feet one-inch and with a three-and one-half foot reach. He could reach over ten feet, which is as tall as a room ceiling. Spring and baseball time are here. The baseball coach asked, "Can you hit, run, throw and catch?" Booker said, "I guess I can. I am thinking I did when on the basketball and football teams. It seems like I can. I'll try it." The coach said, "I want you to hold his baseball. Carry it with you at all times. Wherever you go make sure this baseball is with you. This baseball will be your best friend or your worst enemy this summer."

Then the tests began as usual. He could throw further and faster than any other man on the team. That didn't mean he could be a great pitcher—just fast. Of course, as usual, all eyes were upon him by the teams and observers in the stands. Oh, my yes, the various college and university team coaches, as well as scouts from a number of schools, were watching him. Many fans came for the first few games and then they stopped coming. It's always the same. Booker was the pitcher and learned the throws. No one could swing the bat fast enough to hit anything he threw across the plate! When hitting, his eye coordination was the speed of the ball coming at him and allowed him to hit more home runs than the team had ever experienced. It was always zero points for the opposing team and many, many points for us. Near mid-season the rules committee knew that the revenue for games must resume or there would be no baseball. So, they said, "Booker, with a heavy heart, would you take an interest in track and field and let another pitcher assume you job?" He said, "Yes to the board and to the coach and to the players. I will happily do so because I am kind of bored with baseball."

Now Booker is a summer senior and he is seven feet one-inch tall and going out for many track and field events and will participate in all of them.

It was the same procedure and that summer he had the change to compete. He learned how to throw the javelin and won all of the contests. He learned how to place the shot and won every contest. He ran every race in nine seconds and never lost a race. He could easily pole vault a foot or two above the opponents score and never lost a contest or a relay. His speed would compensate for slower runners.

High hurdles were an easy win because of his ability to run and his speed. Easy win! It became known that if a team was going to participate in a track and field event with Booker competing, the team should plan on receiving the silver medal or not compete at all, because Booker had the gold medal already locked up.

He was seven feet and one and one-half inches when he graduated from high school at the age of fifteen. If he had the words in front of him, the moral to his high school years was that it is not a fulfilling feeling if you always win and never lose. It is not always winning but how you play the game. It takes both for the most fulfillment.

Booker, our very tall, thin man had a scholarship to Kentucky University for his freshman and sophomore years in college. Booker finally met a tall girl and their mental and physical abilities in many ways mirrored each other.

You can guess that college, much like high school, was much the same in academics as well. The tall, thin Booker's new lover's name was Michelle Hensen. Folks thought they were a handsome pair. So, it was no surprise that Michelle and Booker graduated with honors in their senior year. He finally became nineteen and proposed to Michelle. It was no surprise when she said yes.

Booker, our tall, thin man has so many other skills. It will take a page or two to relate the. His love for adventure was not yet quelled. Michele and his first year of marriage was not exactly exciting. It was even boring. They agreed to a quiet separation so she could do the things she wanted and the same for him. Michelle had an insatiable appetite for knowledge, so she continued her scholastic endeavor to become a teacher. Booker and Michelle lovingly separated. They both hurt for a while but kept in touch. It was just five years later when Michelle and Booker met on a plane. She was a professional teacher of law and Booker was a policeman practicing law. Booker became a first line policeman for his skills in offensive weapons and for his courage. His height of seven foot one and one-half inches created a formidable figure when facing criminals. They looked at each other and Booker said, "My God Michelle, I still have feelings for you. Do you feel the same? We are only separated. May we try again?" Right after we hugged Michelle said, "I secretly have been hoping that this would happen. My God Booker—Do I love you!"

Before I close, I would love for you to know a little bit more about Booker's relationship with the birds and the trees. When Booker stood on his large beautiful deck attached to the rear of his home, he found that there were an unusual number of birds in the many trees that grew on his property. Soon he noticed that the birds were sitting on the rail of his deck. Little birds have an innate sense if they are near a friend or foe. Maybe that is why so many perched on the rail of his back deck and even ate from his hands. The red birds, the blue birds and the orioles weren't quite that trusting, but the wee humming birds, sparrows and finches each looked forward to a handout by eating feed from Booker's hand.

Booker stretched out his arm reaching four feet and birds lit upon it just to see what this unusual thing could be. They sensed that there was no need to be alarmed in his presence. They were perched on something that was not a tree. The fact that the bird feeders were attached to the rail nearby helped create this bird sanctuary. Booker's arms were not considered unpleasant to the many birds that could reach them with a flap or two of their wings. Birds of all kinds came and went, sometimes sitting on Booker's shoulders or arms. There were many more little birds, wrens, sparrows and finches that suddenly felt the need to be with Mr. Booker. They sat on his rail and on his arm chair. In fact, they were everywhere enjoying the food that Booker was so thoughtful to place for them to enjoy in his feeders. These were singing birds, big and small that were considered to be heard by the neighbors who sought to see those many birds that flew about and sang apparently to Mr. Booker T. T. Masters.

They were not just a few. There were many birds of all kinds in the neighborhood that sat anywhere they could when Booker stood. Booker loved to lounge in his chair and have the birds tweet their little songs of pleasure.

It was a thing to behold and newspaper people came to take pictures of this most unusual affair that Booker had with all these birds of the area. Indeed, we think that this is one more treasure that Mr. Booker T. T. Masters enjoyed. His height would enthrall the many birds.

Dogs of the area felt they needed to know all the happenings. They crept upon the deck and growled and snarled at Booker for they felt threatened by this huge man. But as soon as Booker reached down and scratched their ears and back, they succumbed to him just as the birds did. They wanted to be near or around him. Now the little dogs came too. They felt they no longer had to worry when the big dogs were about. They felt a sense of security when Booker was near. The cats stayed away from the entire neighborhood even though they had a craving to visit those birds. The cats could not tolerate the nearness of so many dogs.

Booker was never so happy as when his little birds and his dogs all sat about as he was resting on his lounge or sitting in his chair under his umbrella. There was a unification of birds and dogs with that very tall, thin man that loved to relax on his deck overseeing the trees and the watery cove at the back of his house. His deck had become a menagerie!!

A MAGIC MOMENT

BY

WILLIAM L. MILBORN

A MAGIC MOMENT

The sidewalk felt more like iron as I sat against the wall on my well-worn whoopie cushion. I think the "whoopie" had left that cushion some time ago. You guessed it…I'm seen by all who pass me every day as a poor bum begging for coin. Pardon me while I adjust this damn cushion and use this bandana to wipe the sweat from my brow. Okay, to begin with I am not a beggar. I'm one who creates happiness and a feeling of self-worth as they drop coins into my bright yellow basket. It was bright and could be seen and it is round with six-inch total sides. I have a metallic plate in the bottom of my rather large yellow basket which allows me to receive a contribution and know its denomination.

With eyes closed, I can count the money from the various sound coins make when dropping into my basket. We so-called pan-handlers never use pans or beg or reach out for help, like those real beggars did when saying "alms for the poor". No siree, there are only allotted so many of us in the city. We pay for a license for a specific place where we can do our business. We even pay taxes. Some of us are married with children and the wives work. Some of us do rather well depending on the location that we are given. It is a privilege to represent our service. That's right…I said a service. Think about it–you felt it. Every person who donates or gives has a good feeling about themselves. It's almost an ego trip. We in our business are doing a service in providing happiness to those who place or drop money of any denomination in my bright yellow basket.

Some use hats to place before them, and some use coffee cans. Many a person that gives away money will feel better for it.

There are skills and knowledge necessary to become a professional receiver of coin. First, you lower yourself as much as you possibly can in sitting in your location. You never raise your head and you mostly look downwards and be subservient. Just think of yourself as a household pet. Look as though you are in deep sorrow. You will never make it if you carry too much pride.

To do this, only speak with a simple "thank you sir" or "thank you ma'am" after a donation. Another rule is to never stand at your location because you may appear as a person who is a possible threat. Right now, I am squatting because my bottom needs to come off that hard cement. A major reminder is that you will be called a bum, beggar, worthless and told to get a job. They might say, "you offend me", and "get off the street", or "you are a do nothing". Just hang your head low and then those same people who are being hateful to you will drop coins into your hat or basket.

Like the guy who waved and walked by and said, "Oh my—oh my….a-tisket-a-tasket, we found a yellow basket" Guess what? He dropped a dollar!! I loved to see currency floating down into my yellow basket.

It was an extra warm afternoon since the heat of the sun bounced off the side of the building and pavement. But then that's part of the hazard of my profession. I get it in the hot days and fall and winter too. I do try to shorten my hours in stormy, rainy, cold or generally bad weather. Before I continue with the heart and fun of the story, I will say that most of us have no homes and have only girl friends doing the same business.

At night there are dumpsters, elevator shafts, and a lot of cardboard to make sleeping tolerable. On an especially good day we can stay in a local mission a few blocks away. Some cost two dollars a night and a few are free to stay in. Fine restaurants in the area—believe it or not—are kind enough to lay out leftovers or food in back of their restaurants.

Other than that, further away from the casino and the hotel, there are tamale stands and taco stands we can get our fill from under two dollars. That, of course, is a treat since our dollars mean so much. Did I mention that as I sit here alongside this hotel building, I cannot sit close to the entrance of any business? I am not allowed.

I am fortunate to have a prime location across the street from the casino in our town. That casino has more than once caused me some regret I having tried my luck at their nickel and dime slot machines. Whenever I got a little ahead, I was always putting it back in to win more. It just never happens that way.

It is now twilight and my experience that donors to my yellow basket are fewer and far between at this time of day. I will quit for the day and turn my back to the street and count my earnings. Well, well, another donor just as I quit for the day. This was the last person that would contribute that day. He was a well-dressed gentleman who leaned down to my yellow basket and placed a ten-dollar bill in it. As he stood, I said, "Sir, I think you are making a mistake…this is a ten-dollar bill." He said, "I certainly did." He took the ten-dollar bill back and put a one-hundred- dollar bill directly into my hand. He said, "Here, you are an honest man. Just a moment." He reached into his suit pocket and said, "Here is a weekend room and cash value coupons along with breakfast amounting to two hundred dollars from the casino for you. I said, "Are you sure? What can I say?" He said, "Not a thing dear fellow." Then he went to the curb where a car pulled up with a chauffeur. He stepped into the car and said loudly, "My name is Garret!"

I thought what a magic moment this has been. I remember while sleeping in the bus depot, the T.V. was showing the movie about a boy who had found a golden ticket to some adventure. I can't recall any given day where I had a hundred and some dollars to put in my pants pocket. I had spent part of many an evening or early morning curled up in a large chair in a very large casino check-in room. Now, I would be checking in myself for Friday, Saturday, and Sunday night. I am going to live in a shower and watch a lot of television and maybe, once again, try my luck at this huge casino.

At least I will not have to curl up in a bus or train station waiting room where I would be commonly told to please leave. I went to the hotel to redeem my free rooms. I stood behind a man checking in and moved close to the counter after he left to check in myself. I stood close to the counter to conceal and cover up these old raggedy pants and fairly dirty sweater I was wearing. My hair was not combed well. The desk clerk looked at me then nodded to the room manager who walked briskly to where I was standing and said to me, "Where did you get the weekend coupon?"

I said, "A man called Garret." The room manager said, "What was your job with him sir?" I said, "Well, it was not just for him, but for a special contribution for what I was doing in representing the poor people. It is for the betterment of the poor people." He said, "Garret is one of my finest customers. Absolutely! Check this man in. By the way, are you a man of means? Do you want a credit voucher under Mr. Garrets' name?" I said, "You will have to ask him and let me know if he says yes." The room manager said, "Let me call his office and see if he wants to give that to you and what will be the limit on the voucher. Please wait!" A few minutes later, the answer came. Mr. Garrett said, "The voucher is to be for one thousand dollars. When that is used call me again."

I then slipped my hand into my pocket and pulled out my one-hundred-dollar bill and transferred it to my shirt pocket. I could see that they saw that I had money. The manager said, "Have a good weekend sir!"

I was given a room key. What a fine room it was. It was a suite. I am going to have my friends from the street come visit me and maybe sleep over. Key in hand, the manager said, "Your luggage sir?" I said, "I think Mr. Garrett's chauffeur will be bringing that up to my room as soon as I call him and tell him where." The truth is I had no luggage just a box. The manager said, "Have a good week. See you Monday morning when you check out. Here is your voucher for Thursday through Monday's breakfast, lunch and dinner. The charge will be the same. You can have it in the café or in your room. Your beverages will be charged to your voucher. All this will be paid for by the marketing department." Finally, I calculated how much money I had. I had $1300.00 dollars to spend. How long would these magic moments continue?

I found myself walking on beautiful carpet to an elevator. I went past the elevator because I saw a small clothing store. I entered and found myself three shirts and three pants on sale. I also found a belt and a pair of loafers. The bill came to $600.00 dollars of my cash. I asked them, since I was a guest, would they give me a pair of socks for a discount. The clerk looked at me and said, "Here are three pair on us!" And he slipped them into my paper bag. The clothes were given to me on a hanger and in plastic. I said to myself, "I never had this many new clothes and shoes all at once." I couldn't recall that having ever happened to me before, except that which was given me by my mom and dad before they went to the big city in the sky. The clothing salesman said, "Excuse me, I must make a phone call." I saw the way he stared at me and I could see that I looked to him like I was a vagabond. Soon the call was received and he said, "Sir, Mr. Garrett has said there will be no charge for your clothes and to provide you with three jackets and a dozen handkerchiefs as well. You may also pick out several ties to coordinate with your clothes." I said, "Thank you for the phone call you made to Mr. Garrett." The manager said, "Oh, you're not the first one Mr. Garrett has taken a liking to and provided clothing." I could tell he was jealous.

Now off to the elevator where I traveled to the top floor of suites. I left the elevator and walked to my room. I opened the door and there before me was a large suite. I said out loud, "I guess I am going to live like a king until Monday morning." There was a note on the inside of the door saying to place laundry in a plastic bag and put it outside the door. They will be cleaned, ironed and delivered the following morning. Well, that is one service I am not going to accept. I needed them to look worn and a little dirty to fit in with my street profession. But I did quickly divest myself of every stitch and streaked to the bathroom and gasped when I saw that magnificent huge tub. It was big enough to swim in I swear! I drew myself a hot bath and had a choice of soaps, oils and fragrances to wash and to anoint my body. The water remained warm and I lounged in spacious sweet-smelling warm water in that tub for three hours. Finally, I lifted myself from the tub onto plush bathroom carpet and took a full-length bath towel from the counter and wrapped it around myself. My hands were puckered from having laid in the water so long. In that towel I sped to the bed and threw myself in the middle of it. Four could have easily slept in the bed. I rolled around on the plush bed covers until I was totally dry. I dare not sleep for I probably wouldn't awake until morning.

I thought to myself, "There will be no cardboard for the next three nights." That warm hot bath made me hungry as an old street dog. I said, "I'll have a good dinner and do a little gambling tonight." Precious little gambling will I do with the few free vouchers and a little limited cash that I had.

That's okay because I had bar privileges to fill in extra time in tasting drinks I always wanted to try. There will be no wine tonight. I want to try whiskey, rum, Bloody Marys, Margueritas, Tom Collins, daiquiris, brandy and champagne. All those drinks I heard about in the movies. I made a beeline for my new clothes hanging in the spacious closet—a closet big enough to live in. My three shirts, pants, coats, and ties seemed lost on all those empty racks. Then it hit me…I forgot to buy some underwear. I would not put on the old ones since I was so clean. I did take my dirty underwear and place them in the bathroom sink and covered them with hot water. Then I dumped a bottle of soap and beat them up and down with a bath brush and left them to soak. Well, I will go without underwear tonight, but I will remember to get some on the way back to the room…my palace. I wondered if I called room service and asked them if they could deliver three pair of size 36 shorts to my room tomorrow and put them on my account. I thought to myself, "What a strange thing to do!!"

I took a small towel and made it into a kind of diaper and opened a drawer full of things such as pens, pencils, and pins. I pinned that self-made diaper on so I wouldn't eventually wet or soil my pants. If I had a problem with incontinence, I would not soil my beautiful new pants.

Finally, I slipped on one of my new pair of pants…those black pants… along with a gray stripped long sleeve shirt made of cotton. I looked like a casual gambler with no tie. So, I added a tie. I put a black bow tie on just to be classy. A black bow tie would allow my gray stripped shirt to stand out. I am beautiful and smell oh so good. I looked beautiful and all the girls would be at my side tonight.

With a key in my pocket and a billfold in my britches, I left reluctantly this suite of dreams and made my way to the dining room which was set aside for the elite and big spenders. I needed no money for meals for the weekend. Since all the meals were courtesy of Mr. Garrett, I did not have to pay. I ordered a porterhouse steak with a mountain of French fries. I also had hot buns with a simple salad. I had ordered escargot, which I had always wanted to try, as an appetizer.

I ordered warm rum. The rum came first and I downed it very quickly. Then I waited for my server. He marched to my table with a large silver tray holding my feast. With a great flourishing gesture, he placed each item before me, including napkins and silverware. Even before he left, I felt myself drooling.

I savored every bite of the once-in-a-lifetime meal. I even like this escargot, whatever they were, I didn't know. I must ask… no…it would make me sound like a rube.

The zings and dings of the music of the casino played their sounds to betting customers. It was as usual pretty music to me. As I was ready to walk out of the dining room, I felt as if I had stolen something, since I had not paid for my meal. Just as I stood ready to leave, my fancy dressed waiter walked up to me and said, "Sir, you haven't had your dessert yet." I said, "Oh yes!" I trembled at the thought that I was about to miss a favorite part of the meal. "What should I have?" I asked in a most intelligent voice, "What would you recommend?" The waiter said, "Warm cherries jubilee spread over cheesecake and honey cakes with soft ice-cream surrounding this delightful course. You may also take this little box of fudge with you when you leave!" I thought, "Oh my God!" I indeed was speechless. I sat again while his associate cleaned the table. He placed a pretty clean open napkin before me on which they were to place my dessert. I waited and stared at the yellow and red rose floating in blue water in a shallow bowl on the table covered in gold leaf.

It finally came…the cous-de-gras. Again, it was presented with much flair. The waiter said, "Sir, this is one of our finest desserts." I saw the cherries jubilee which was doused with rum and fire set to it. It quickly burst into flames and then it went out. The cherries in sauce were poured over the cheesecake and honey cakes. The ice cream was then placed around the dessert and sprinkled with pecans.

I loosened my belt two notches after I had consumed that mammoth dessert. I said the four words that I never say, "I have had enough!"

The waiter walked up to me and said, "Is there anything further, Sir?" I said, "Yes, wrap up the leftovers so that I may give them to my dog!" The waiter said, "Sir, what leftovers?" I said, "Alright then, please have another porterhouse steak prepared only. I will come back to pick it up before I return to my suite. Oh yes, put $20.00 as a tip on that bill before you present it to the hotel for payment. Thank you, Sir!" The waiter said, "Sir, we normally receive 20 percent and that would make the tip $40.00." I thought to myself, "How long would it take on the street for me to make $40.00?"

I said, "Consider it done. Put it on the bill!" He died. I signed then I turned and directed my feet towards the casino and the sounds of the jingling coins and the bells and whistles of the casino machines.

My free play amounted to $200.00 in vouchers. I went to the coin cage and transferred the money to a card which I will insert for a game play. I would have taken money but that is not allowed. These are free play privileges. I thought if this is free play, I will bet a $1.00 per play for any game on the gambling floor. I noticed the gamblers who pay more get more. Those who spend a dollar per play receive better odds and more wins than those who play five, ten, or twenty-five cents. My plan is to put a dollar in every slot machine in hopes of winning a big payoff.

I won and I lost, and after losing I won, then I lost, but I noticed that even with the winning there was a dwindling on the amount remaining on the cash card. I thought, "Well, it's free play and I am having fun." It was really late when I played the "sun and moon" machine near the entry and exit door. Then who should I see just inside the door? It was Bernice, my street girlfriend. I gave her a hug and said, "I want you to join me tonight in my suite along with four of our friends on our side of the street."

I said, "Tell your friends Joyce, Anna, Dave, and Tony it's paid for and to come to this door and I will take them to our suite where you will have a couple of nights in great comfort…bathing, bed…the works. I will even have room service deliver food and beverages. I know for a fact I will be taking to the room a porterhouse steak. Tell them to adjust their clothing and come their hair so as not to look out of place." It was twenty minutes before Joyce brought our friends to the door. We briskly and without much ado made our way to the hall elevator and escaped to the second floor where I walked them to the suite. I opened the door and I had them individually walk into the beautiful place. They were stunned.

They said, "You mean you will let us sleep here tonight?" Grab pillows, it will be more comfortable than the dumpster or a two-dollar mission. They all said, "Hooray!" I said, "When deliveries are made, I want you to hide so no one will know you are here. In doing this, I may be breaking a hotel rule or policy. Like me, you will probably want to take baths. There is room for more than one in the tub. I prefer that you bathe one at a time. You may draw fresh bath water each time. Girls first. There are three sinks in that bathroom so the girls can wash their hair and then their clothes.

There is a stack of body-length towels for you to wrap yourselves in. Our room has a balcony. After washing your clothes, put them on the balcony to dry. When that is completed, you may pick the chair or couch you prefer. There are two couches and six reclining chairs and two beds. Everyone will have to lay close to their sleeping spots which will be yours until Monday morning. When the women are through, each of you men may draw straws for where you may sleep and take your separate baths in the bathroom. Don't worry, there is plenty of hot water for each of you to enjoy. You may take a private bath. There is shaving soap and shower soap and lotion for men and women. So, live it up and enjoy until Monday!

Every morning I understood that the cleaning ladies would come by and resupply, but not until ten o'clock. This gives you time to have breakfast and dress before nine a.m. Then you can be off to the casino before they arrive. Room service will supply all the breakfast food you want. They don't care what is ordered. They all get paid. So be up by seven a.m. and dressed. Your clothes on the balcony will be dry by morning.

I have seen a towel cart in the hallway and right now I will go there and wheel that cart to our door and all of you take all the towels. I will then take the empty cart and push it to the end of the hall. The maid will wonder where the towels went, but they will go to a large hall closet and replenish their supply.

We will have an early breakfast here by eight a.m. There will be omelets, sausage, bacon and milk and flapjacks. I want you properly dressed with your hair combed and looking as nice as you can. Enjoy your time in the casino. Don't get caught and order room service at your convenience. You have no money to gamble with. They all said, "Who says so?" I said, "Okay make your money last and enjoy. If questioned by a floor manager as to who you are, say you are a friend of mine. Garrett, who is a very rich man, owns this hotel and casino. Everyone seems to know him. You are only here because Mr. Garrett likes me and has given me a large credit voucher to pay for what we spend. We will get together several times during the day so you can enjoy your free drinks on Mr. Garrett."

He knows you work the streets where his hotel operates. Please don't go broke when gambling. Have fun with the nickel and dime machines. I have the money he gave me that I will share with you. There are five of you and each of you will get $50.00 to play with. Good luck! I will hide the key card on the top of the door frame. I will use chewing gum to hold it in place. Do not approach me anywhere in the casino.

I do not want to be watched as to what I play or how I play on these one-armed bandits. I've had breakfast and am leaving you. I will see you back in the room later and I'll have a big surprise for all of you later. No arguing, fighting or hanky-panky with the girls or you will dishonor my invitation.

I left with a little anxiety as to what my friends would be up to, but that was then and this is now and it is their nature to be adventuresome or they would not be street people like myself.

I now had two floors of gaming to try out. Same old thing—win some and lose some!!

I wanted to extend my play on the slots to part of Saturday and Sunday. The next afternoon I ordered from the kitchen delivery six T-bone steaks, macaroni and cheese, and shrimp, or surf and turf, for my fine guests and myself. The six orders were placed including hot rolls and dessert of cherry cheesecake. I had them add a substantial tip to the bill and I had it delivered to my suite at six p.m. Now for the surprise...I went to the bar and put on the account two one-half gallons of rum and a small commercial keg of beer. In addition, I ordered chips and dips.

I so enjoyed wandering about on the floor of that casino watching people win and lose.

It was about 5:00 p.m. Saturday when I headed back to the suite. I was actually tired. Gambling is work. It makes you think too much. I found the card key above the door mantle. I went in and everyone was there. Joyce says, "You can't play without money!" I said, "I said "I know...I know, but I think we all will just enjoy this little palace of mine!" Joyce said, "Watching T.V. on that giant screen is a thrill!" I asked, "What are you watching?" She said, "We are watching a show called 'Chicago', and we just love it."

All five of my friends were lounging all over the living room and the floor and they were possessed by that big screen T.V. I said, "Is everyone broke?"

"Never mind now Billy. We didn't have that much to lose in the first place and look at the joy we experienced in betting and the bed and breakfast." I said, "You ain't seen nothin' yet!" Then came a rapping at our door. I said, "I wonder who that can be?" I opened the door and the delivery was here with the gallons of booze and beer and chips and dips. They all jumped to their feet. I had it all set up on the big dining room table. There were glasses and mugs, napkins and olives and large insulated silver ice containers full of ice cubes. The hotel beverage manager looked it all over and also at my friends and said, "Are you sure that is enough Sir?" I said, "Well, I don't know!" He said, "But, there is no wine sir." I thought, "Once a wino always a wino. Joyce, what kind of wine would you like? She said, "I would like peach wine, strawberry and grape wine." I said, "Sir, bring that wine along with a mix for some of this good drink." He said, "Of course, we will bring up a case of cola and 7-up. Now will that be all sir?" I said, "I really don't know." He said, "Beverage service ends at 10:00 p.m." I said, "So soon?" He said, "Yes Sir." He handed me a plate with a bill o it. I said, "I thought this was part of the courtesy of this trip paid for my Mr. Garrett." He said, "It is but I have to account for it. Add twenty-five dollars in tips." My friends unanimously said, "That much?" I said, "Aye!" The beverage manager left the room and the drinking began in earnest. The movie was turned to a musical channel and the singing began! I said, "No…no…We can't make that kind of noise. You will have to just listen and sing quietly!" I joined this merriment with my friends and said,

"My street friends, do you hear that rapping at the door? Well, this is the second part of my surprise for you. I opened the door and in came a trail of food wagons. They were loaded with sizzling steaks with mounds of crinkle cut French fries and simple salad, and mac-n-cheese. The waiter cleared the dining room table and placed all of our food on the table and the remaining beverages were placed on a delivery cart. As soon as the food was put on the dining room table, we were happy. There were just six chairs at that table. My friends insisted I be seated at the front end of the table.

Dave sat at the other end of this long table and took his little mini Bible from his pocket. He said Grace and pronounced a small prayer and blessed each of us. We ma be poor in money but much endowed in our prayers to our creator. Two hours later the food service staff entered to remove all the dishware. Everyone asked for a "to go" box and not a crumb was left or a bottle of beverage. All the food and condiments were cleared while quiet music played on as everyone now needed to sleep off the entertainment.

What a sight the maids did see when they entered the suite the next morning to clean. I said with one open eye, "The party's over ladies. We will stay out of the way and we will just continue to sleep." The three cleaning ladies laughed and said, "No problem!" After awakening, no one had any interest for breakfast but did wish for an urn of coffee. I said, "That is the last of the feast that I am supplying, except for hamburgers and fries tonight."

I said, "Today you may do what you choose—wander around at the casino—get free drinks at the bar—watch T.V. or get your clothes all cleaned up. As you know, tomorrow morning will be early check-out time. We must be out by 9:00 a.m."

I also said, "Don't forget to take all the mini soaps, shampoos, and lotions you have been collecting for three days at least. The maids somehow know our situation and have been leaving us toothpaste, shampoo, soaps, and lotion and deodorants. Put them in your little tote bags and wander out tomorrow morning. I'll have a large urn of coffee sent along with sweet rolls and doughnuts delivered to our room for you to have before leaving. Taking a towel or one of those pretty bathrobes is tempting, I know, but let's don't do it."

For me, I am going to sit at a poker table for most of the day and play only hands that appear to be "bet" hands and have the best odds for winning.

Everybody went their separate ways for the day and we were all back in the suite by 6:00 p.m. Dave and Tony didn't even leave the suite. They watched the T.V. I said, "Put the news or music on guys and clean the tables because we are about to get a pile of all-American fast food. They will bring hamburgers and hot dogs and a bunch of curly fries, plus three large pizzas and plenty of sliced onions, two jars of pickles, one sweet and one dill spears. Only a keg of beer tonight and one-half bottle of good old wino wine and a big jar of jalapeno peppers. Remember, get up early. We will be leaving in the morning and you had better schedule the bathroom privileges tonight because even that large bathroom with three sinks and a shower and the bath tub will be pressed to give us all the time we need." I heard a knocking at the door and it was the hotel food service people. I opened the door and there came in trays on a food wagon and beverages and beer and wine and our fast food. There were several large pitchers of ice water as well.

We listened to music and drank as long as we dared. I asked our food service manager, "Can you pick all of this stuff up in the morning after we leave at 9:00 a.m.?" He said, "No, we can't do that! But we won't pick up until 11:00 p.m. Best I can do! Rules you know!" We all had a great time and watched for the second time that song and dance musical called "Chicago".

My friends were like good obedient soldiers for they were out of the room taking everything that wasn't nailed down, including food and drinks that they packed away before the food service cleared the room last night. My friends even straightened up the place.

With my suite key in hand and my little suit case provided by Mr. Garrett, I packed my new clothing and I headed for check-out. Of course, I was dressed down to look the part for accepting street donations as I would look outside beside the hotel wall. I thought how strange… from the suite to the street.

I rattled a few silver dollars in my pocket as I turned in my suite key. I asked, "By the way, what were the total charges for my weekend with you?" The clerk said, "The bill, including tips, was $3,234.50!" I said, "How much?!" He shouted back giving me a look of consternation and said, "I am sure Mr. Garrett had not planned on picking up this sizable amount, but of course he will. He will because it is his hotel!" I felt guilty as I headed towards the casino exit which was beautiful to impress money gamblers. I jangled those silver dollars in my pocket one more time and then I saw that huge "volcano" machine next to the entrance. It occasionally blew a puff of smoke and continued a growling and rumbling and shaking of a volcano sound. It was tall and the guests loved to play this machine and even have their pictures taken with it. It was quite a show piece! Don't think any one expected to win as they stood on a little platform and placed their two dollars into that twelve-foot tall machine. The machine was structured and painted to look just like a volcano. Even though it would cost two dollars to play, it was a high-class slot machine. I said, "Why not?" I stepped up onto that little platform and with a feeling that since I had thrown all my money away into this sea of machines, I should drop two more silver dollars into this one. I had a feeling of indifference at putting two of my silver dollars into the gigantic beast of a volcano.

I faced the large dollar slot and placed two silver dollars into it. Then I pressed it forward and it made a shrill whirring sound like a whistle. Then I did the same thing with my second silver dollar. I even said, "Goodbye" to them and slammed the receiver bar closed. Then it made a chugging sound. The platform shook and shook and then there was a gigantic explosion as this volcano blew red confetti high into the air and it sprinkled down everywhere! A siren went off, a whistle went off and the star-spangled banner played. Frankly, it was scary. Suddenly, people were cheering all around me. The floor manager came running. The manager said, "I thought I would never see that machine pay. For two and a half years it has been swallowing and eating the gamblers money and you, poor beggar, have won!!! You can get some new clothes. New everything you want for you have just won two million dollars! That is two million dollars! I think my math is right on that!!"

People were congratulating me. They were patting me on the back and shaking my hand and then I said, "Look who's coming. The casino owner himself!" He walked up close to me as the rumbling stopped and the stage stopped shaking. He said, "I know you! You are a good man. Good fortune always comes back again and again to a good man. Well this is a magic moment for you Billy." I said, "How did you know my name?" He said, "I have been signing those vouchers and tickets since you have been here!"

I stepped down from the vibrating volcano platform onto the casino floor. I said, "Thank you Mr. Garrett. I can't believe this day. I think I am dreaming." He pinched me on the arm and said, "Feel that? You're not dreaming! I had this feeling too Billy, when the many things led up to my suddenly owning this casino." Mr. Garrett threw an arm around my shoulder and said, "We are going to my office. We have got to talk!"

There I was sitting across the desk in Mr. Garrett's office. The office was ornate with antiques of every sort. They were on shelves standing on the floor and overhead. Mr. Garrett plopped down behind his massive oaken desk. I sat in his leather chair across from him. He said, "Billy, you are my friend and you know that I am. The casino makes a fortune during the year, even after winning payouts and payments to four managers, staff and kitchen expenses, as well as housekeeping expenses. I am continuously asked for more money than I can spend, but I try. Now this is a strange predicament.

All of the lawyers know about the two million dollars, my clients, customers, and all of my staff know it, and now I must pay it. Billy, I DO NOT have two million dollars in cash to pay you today, even if that is what the gaming commission requires. The rule is that the payout must be made the day the customer wins it.

The casino is a corporation and a private ownership. It is not listed on the New York Exchange or any other exchange. So, I cannot give you stock as part of your win, but I can do something that I have never done and that is to give you a percentage of the ownership in this casino. In the long run it would be to my advantage to pay you off. The casino does not have two million dollars on had to make such a payout. It's just that damn machine decided to cough up this big win all of a sudden rather than make moderate wins over the last three years.

I have one million in cash that we can put in your checking and savings accounts in your bank and offer to sell you the balance of your winnings after taxes toward the purchase of part ownership in this money-making casino. You see the percentage I sell you perhaps cannot be as much as you would like, but both the state, federal and county tax commissioners want a piece of the action by way of taxing the profits. Let's say that I reluctantly will have my attorneys draw up your part of the ownership in this business. I am thinking one and one-half million will be the balance of your winnings after taxes. The money will be placed in your savings and checking accounts as you would like it."

I asked, "Mr. Garrett, what is your first name?" He said, "My name is Charles Garrett…think of Charlie the Tuna. Think of me as one of those rags to riches people that will one day tell you about his trip. Well Billy?" I said, "May I call you Charlie?" He said, "Yes Billy, you may call me Charlie." As I spoke the first word, I had one of my epiphanys again.

I have a need to help others just like you. I want very much to own that mission house a few blocks away from this casino. I want to offer meals and a place to sleep for those that are on the street. You may call them pan-handlers or bums, beggars or losers, but Sir, you will find that each has a story to tell. They may have a physical disability or mental disability. They may have been injured in the service. Some never had an opportunity to learn a trade or go to school. Some were abandoned as a child but Charlie, like us, well we are all God's children.

We sat in silence and Charlie had hung his head low. I thought he was sad and crying but no–Charlie was thinking.

He said, "Let's do this. Instead of me trying to hire you in some job here, let me buy that mission and refurbish it so that every room has a bath. We can hire a food server team so we may take care of that small army of people that need help. We will start with sixty rooms."

"Charlie, you would do that?" He said, "Yes I will. It would probably make me feel good. Just thinking about it makes me feel good, not to speak of that large amount of taxes I could write off for expenses in providing this charity. I still think that I want you to give these folks some incentive to seek this bed and board." I said, "I agree!"

It will be three dollars a day and two dollars a day for the people who use prosthetics and handicapped. Because of the tax write off I could easily take care of simple needs for anyone who chooses to stay at your mission house.

This mission is to feed and provide shelter and a clean place to sleep with fresh linens. It will not require religious services. "Good idea Billy. So be it!" He continued, "Billy, you realize you will be paying some pretty good taxes yourself?" I said, "Now I do!" Garrett said, "Do you know what nine percent of your one and one-half million-dollar ownership is on this place?" I said, "No, tell me". He said, "It is one hundred thirty-five thousand plus interest from your bank savings account. Now Billy I expect you to pay a percentage of your new found wealth to pay for city, state, and county business taxes. Out of the one and one-half million, you will only own one sixth of the value of this business. I will let you know what your taxes will be as soon as I can.

Now Billy, my friend, I will run the casino end of our business and you can manage the Good Will portion of our business. Keep records of all that you spend for that mission because it can be deductible.

All you need is a journal for that and my accountant will give you that. Then give the receipts to Mr. Column, our accountant, two days prior to the end of the month. Contracts for your share of the casino and contracts for our mission objectives will be ready for you to sign Friday morning by 9:00 a.m. Billy, you need to go the City Bank down the street and get your checking and savings account book and consider yourself a business man, doing good for your community. Just as it has been your dream all along and you didn't know it. Billy, you are a good honest caring human being. I am proud to know you."

I said, "Charlie what can a man say to that? I will say that my friends you entertained for the weekend told me go give you a big thank you if ever I were to see you. The first thing I am going to do is get my checkbook and write a check to our casino for the $3,432.50 that I spent this weekend for myself and my friends. I would not feel right if I didn't repay this since I know I overspent the amount you probably intended. Goodbye Charlie. I will see you Friday."

Charlie said, "Go down and tell all of your friends what they can look forward to when the renovations are completed. Until then, they will only sleep and eat here on your dime! Charlie laughed and said, Oh sweet revenge!"

To the bank I went and paid the hotel bill for my five closest friends... my street friends. They could not believe my second windfall. I would own a mission for them to spend their nights and the food service that would provide food twelve hours a day. Tony said that we will continue what we do and I said, "Fine, you are still going to pay three dollars a day for bed, bath and clean sheets and food." My friends still want to continue their professions on the street.

They all agreed it was a gift and I looked at my friends and I felt some were handicapped and a bit uneasy in securing their donations in their hats, coffee cans or baskets, because Dave wore a synthetic leg brace and had another standing by his place where he sat. Mike always wore that eye patch on his left or right eye or wherever he pleased for the day and Joyce only wore one sock and one shoe on the other foot. She loved it when people would ask, "Where is your other shoe?" And she would say it was either a cat, dog, rat or some other critter that ran away with it. One was with child. We knew she had a little pillow under her dress and it would indicate her condition. She was really going to have a child.

I am going to keep my little yellow basket. It had good memories for me and it was part of that "magic moment" when I took the ten dollars and gave it back to Mr. Garrett suggesting that he made a mistake in giving me too large an amount. He started this dream by giving me a free weekend with food and betting vouchers. I am now going to tour that mission down the street and see all the wonderful things that I can do. These improvements will make a visit there more pleasurable. On the way there I bought a clip board and some sharpie pens, a few pencils and an eraser and a notebook to join the accounting pad which I had already been given by Mr. Garrett's accounting manager.

This whole matter now proclaimed me as a business man and what a success it will be. What "magic moments" there have been this weekend.

As you know, my last name is O'Day and as of this day I have found my leprechaun. His name is Charlie Garrett. His real last name is Charlie Finnigan. I should have known as an Irishman that the special glint in Charlie's eyes suggested he was a leprechaun. It was easy to follow my leprechaun's advice for he will be for me and the advice will be golden. Mr. Charlie Finnigan had found his own "pot of gold" at the end of his rainbow in this casino.

A "SHORT" STORY

BY

WILLIAM L. MILBORN

A "SHORT" STORY

Below five feet five inches, a man is considered short and highly discriminated against. Too short to be a policeman, too short to be a pilot, too short for most management jobs, too short for most women who prefer tall, dark, etc., too short for basketball, too short for most coats and pants (They have to be taken up). Furthermore, it seems being short equates to a man's intelligence and strength. Agreed, we are even too short in that we need a step ladder to do many household repairs (inside or outside).

That word short is applied in so many ways. One is short-handed, or have a short memory, a little short on cash and will pay you shortly. But mostly the word short infers more negative than positive events. Even those who transcribe dictation are taught shorthand. You are told to keep your message short. They have short conversations. Things are short-lived and to-dos are put on the short list.

Why short cake? Go the shortest way. That's okay, especially if you are on a short trip. I may have short falls in my overall character or training. I take a short cut wherever I go and whenever I can. I like short ribs, don't you? Life is short, but we are told that short people live longer lives that tall people–how about that!

I am short of breath. I will take a short break, read short stories, such as this one. I don't have a shortage of friends. The lights went out–must have a "short" in the electrical line. I will catch you shortly, while I take a short moment to think of what I can say next about that nasty little five letter word name "Short"!

I have thought of one more…A short man is thought to have a shorter private part than a tall man or any man of color. It may be true. I am not going to check it out. You may give a girl a long kiss or a short one. Why is it that the loser always draws the short straw?

Well, I am going to pull up my shorts, put on my short pants and lay back in my recliner and just forget about being short.

As I lay in my chair, I am thinking of a short-order cook that I once had in my fast-food drive-in. I recall he was especially good at making short cakes.

I guess I will take a short nap now and dream of being tall so that I may be a basketball star. Did you ever see the short end of a stick! That's all unless you, my short friend, can think of more to add. On, frankly, I have spoken so much in this short story that in order to shorten it I have become short-winded. I already know that I am short sighted. That is why I wear glasses.

For the fun of it, I have left space at the end of this ode for you to name well known famous people that are short!! I would name a few short people but I have such a short memory. It dates me I know…

I will start:

1. Napoleon
2. Edward G. Robinson
3. Jimmy Cagney
4. Humphry Bogart
5. Danny DeVito
6. Mickey Rooney
7. The Seven Dwarves (They hated to be called dwarves)

MY MYNA BIRD
WITH A MIND

BY

WILLIAM L. MILBORN

MY MYNA BIRD WITH A MIND

It was a warm spring day when I quietly opened the screen door and entered my home. Jeanette, my lovely wife, had left the front door open to allow the morning breezes into the house. As usual, she arrived home from her bank teller job before I got home. Everyday Jeanette would then go the bedroom and take a nap. I laid back in my recliner and said to myself, "Me too! A nap will do just fine!" I no sooner drifted off than here came my friend with a thermal cooler full of cans of Miller High Life beer.

He yanked the screen door open and stepped in. Then in a raspy voice came the words, "Come in!", then again, "Come in!" I leaped up and we both froze when we heard it. Joe said, "Is there someone here beside Jeanette?" I said, "No!" Then came that raspy voice saying, "What do ya know Joe? What do ya know Joe?" Joe stared at me and said, "Who is here that knows my name?" I gave him the short neck and said, "No one!!" Joe said, "Now Willie, we heard it." Then again as we stood there we heard, "Come in! Hello! Hello!" followed by "Joe…Joe…Joe!" The voice came from the dining room and in unison we said, "Hello!" back to it.

As we walked to the large dining room, we saw a little stand with a bird cage inhabited by a large beautiful black bird. We said simultaneously, "A bird! No, maybe a parrot, but not an old blackbird." I never heard a blackbird or a parrot speak so distinctly, like a raspy voiced person. The bird continued to repeat, "Come in!…Come in!…Joe! Joe! Joe! What do ya know?"

Then Joe said, "Willie it can't be true. I bet you know a ventriloquist hiding behind a curtain. Willie I am looking at that bird talk to me. It must be a ventriloquist."

Then here came my wife, Jeanette, and she quickly came over to us. She put her hand on my shoulder and said, "What do you think about that bird?" I said, "Where did you get it? Is it ours?" She said, "Yes Willie, it is ours to keep." "Why?", I asked. Jeanette said, "Because it has no other place to go. I can't tell you why! My bank friend gave me the beloved bird. Okay, I will tell you why. The owner of that bird cried when she put that stand and cage into our car. She loved the bird but she gave it to me." I said, "Is that right? Why?" Jeanette said, "I will tell you later. I can't at this moment." I said, "Why the mystery?"

Joe was, by now, practically nose-to-nose with that black bird and waiting to hear his name again in bird talk. That big old blackbird said loudly with his black eyes staring directly into Joe's, "I can talk! Can you fly?" Joe stepped quickly back in awe and said, "This is witchcraft! Someone has turned a human into a bird!" The bird repeated, "I can talk! Can you fly?" Joe found himself answering the bird's questions, "No, I can't fly!" Joe looked at me and said, "I have just spoken to a bird! You know no one at work will believe us." Then Joe asked the bird a question and smiled at me, "Can you fly?" Big bird said, "Joe! Joe! Joe!" Joe asked, "Why big bird?" The bird did not answer but let loose with a song. He sang, "East side, west side, all around the town." Every note was perfect. I said, "Joe, before you faint, let's sit at the table and have one of those beers. Think with drink!

Jeanette said, "Now you've done it!" For no sooner than I said the word "beer" than big bird was thrashing around in his large cage like he was being attacked. We three sat at the table watching the bird until he stopped his crazy tantrum. Now big bird just sat on his swing staring at us with glazed eyes. "Do not say that 'beer' word again." I said, "Honey, do you think he can hear and understand everything we say?" She said, "Maybe...maybe. Now let me give you each a napkin to cover your beverages as you take them from the cooler so the bird can't see the letters spelling out 'beer'." Joe asked, can I bring my family and friends around to see the bird?"

I said, "No Joe, that would certainly start something." I added, "I might as well sell tickets for the number of people that would want to see it and hear it speak. Besides it would make the bird a nervous wreck. I think you and I were enough shock for him in one day. Jeanette, we keep saying 'him'. How do we know that 'he' is not a 'she'!" Jeanette said, "I don't know Willie. What makes the difference?" Then the bird came out of its temporary stupor and said loudly, "Where is that old bird dog?" Again, our mouths flew open and we shook our heads and said, "Are we dreaming?" Now, I spoke to our new friend and said, "Bird, we do not have a hound dog." Then it started making the best sound he could and mimicked laughter and then the bird did a terrible imitation of a hound dog howling. The bird just didn't have the "wind" for it.

We three just sat there at the table and commented on the mystery of it all. I said, "Jeanette, you haven't answered me. Why did your friend Molly give you her beloved bird?" Jeanette said, "I'm not sure she would like me to say, but since the question will never go away, it was because Molly's son would bombard this poor old bird with his empty 'beer' cans. Her son laid on a family couch in her home just across the room where big bird lived in this big cage which was on a stand. Her son, normally a great guy when sober, became a demon when he awoke after he had drunk a six pack of beer! He would grab a shoe, or beer can and rattle the poor bird in his cage. "My friend Molly had seen too much of this abuse and asked me to take the bird. When I agreed, we put it in my car and I brought it home with me for you to discover and be surprised." We three sat until nearly sunset just staring in wonderment and wondering what the bird's future might be. What with my wife and I owning an ornery cat!

It's a matter of keeping them separated or again big bird will become paranoid in fighting with that old cat, which might attack. After all, a cat is a bird's enemy. The bird could have a heart attack, you know.

It has been hours since Joe arrived while this fascinating afternoon has been going on. We are now feeling a little bit high on our beverages. I said, "Remember guys, do not say that word 'b-e-e-r'".

The sun was but a glimmer as we could see it from the dining room through the sliding glass door leading to our patio. I said, "Another surprise, boys! Guess what big bird like to drink?" Joe asked, "Milk?" I said, "Maybe!" Joe said, "Soft drinks?" Then I said, "He doesn't like to see that you know what kind of can. It does love the taste of what is in it. You may give the bird a round of drinks by pouring a 'beer' into that large container you see attached to the cage which maintains a spout leading to its watering hole."

Joe said, "Really? It likes it?" I said, "More like it loves it. I sometimes think it may have the same kind of problem that Molly's son has—in a word—alcoholism!" Joe said, "Ya think so?" I said, "So maybe we shouldn't give it too much since it is relatively small compared to adult humans. Oh yes, when bird becomes hungry you will see it jump onto its drum and start to beat its feet—kind of like a tap dance. Also, you had better feed him because he makes terrible squawking sounds like a boy when he is hungry. Jeanette and I must remember when we are at the store to get an abundance of fruit of any kind, like fresh avocados, fresh strawberries, apples and grapes and don't forget the peaches, pears and bananas. Get everything! Then put it through the large blender and well…drop it into the bird's feeding box and not too much at a time.

I said, "Jeanette, let's call it a night. You still need to cook supper and feed the bird." The bird started feeling lonely and clumsy and he said, "Well, I guess I'll stay home!" This time we laughed and smiled and said, "How funny can that be?"

I said, "I wonder what else he can say?" Jeanette added, "I guess we will have to wait until another day to find out." Joe said, "I can't wait to join you tomorrow evening Willie. I'll bring the beer as usual for we three and the bird too!" Joe left and with the closing of the front door, we wondered how it is that bird would know to say, "Bye! Bye! Bye!"

I said, "Jeanette, give that bird these seedless cherries in that jar over there and try him on several olives without pits." Jeanette did that, covered his cage and we did not expect to hear another word from bird. It had not learned a word for "goodnight". The bird did say "Bye, Bye!" as she covered his cage with a large black cloth that was a cage cover. I said, "Jeanette, shall we have pizza or go out to eat?" She said, "No dear, let's have leftovers tonight. We have bologna, chicken, sliced turkey and all kinds of condiments." I added, "Of course, we'll polish off that shot of brandy and rum that is left." We went to our bedroom with our strange thoughts and all that bird talk we heard that day.

The next morning, I said, "Oh God, it's Saturday. It's play day and go to the store day." Both Jeanette and I slept until nine a.m. First thing we did was go to the dining room to check on bird. Oh my! He was beating his feet on his "dancing" drum. Bird was hungry. I slipped the big black cover from his cage and bird stopped dancing and just stared at me as if he knew where his food was coming from.

I sat and looked at bird. As soon as Jeanette came with bird's breakfast, I said, "Oh, you're not going to feed expensive blueberries to a bird!?" Jeanette said, "I am. He's a member of the family. We will just have to get more for your precious blueberry pie." We too had our breakfast–flapjacks and molasses topped with pecans.

After eating and dishes were done, we were free to do as we pleased. I said, "We will take bird and show him off to our friends at the police station and fire department since they are located next to each other. It will be an easy trip!"

They see a lot of crazy things, but our presentation of bird just may be the craziest thing that they have ever seen. Jeanette said, "Let's do it!" As she unhooded the top of the bird cage and headed for the car. "Bird, you need to get out too!" Five minutes later we entered the Chief's briefing room and placed bird on the table. The chief said, "Willie, Jeanette, what is this? Why did you bring this old black bird to my briefing room?" "You'll see!" I continued, "Please ask your friend the chief of police in the next building to come here with a bunch of officers to witness a miracle."

The chief was seven-foot tall, a massive man! He said, "I will humor you today Willie, because you are my friend and belong to our poker club and my church." How did bird know not to speak until everyone arrived is a mystery. We kept the bird cage cover over his cage so he wouldn't be frightened. When everyone arrived, we opened the curtain and said, "Show time!"

Everyone next door crowded the briefing room the police chief said, "This better not be an April fool's stunt." Then in a perfectly clear, but raspy voice, the bird said, "I can talk. Can you fly?" Everybody went crazy. They all said, "It's a toy! Where is the ventriloquist?" I said, "You all come closer!" All the bird could see were faces all around. It sounded like the bird cleared his throat and sang, "East side, west, side, all around the town!" You could hear a pin drop as everyone saw that bird's beak speak those words. The bird followed up by saying, "Where's that old bird dog?" They all laughed and said, "We just have a dalmation that rides with us." The police chief said, "We have a police dog—several police dogs—but each of them rides with a different officer every day." The police chief then said, "Well, any other surprises?" The bird said, "What do ya know Joe?" Then all those police officers (there were one-half dozen or so) said, "Right here!" The bird said again, "What do ya know Joe?" The bird repeated this several times. They applauded and laughed for they had their names called by a bird. "Has your name ever been called by a bird?"

One of policemen jumped in his car and hit the siren, but bird liked that and immediately responded by making the precise sounds that the police siren made. That bird started whistling and chirping the bird sounds he had heard coming from the trees around our patio. They were beautiful and bird went into one chirping sound after another. The chirping and bird sounds it had heard were now coming from that little black beak of our big bird.

I was glad I had been leaving that patio door open for fresh air. I had no idea the bird was listening to and imitating his feathered friends that he would never meet but could only listen to.

The police chief was recording the beautiful bird sounds. I said, "Everyone, thank you for giving big bird a fun time out." Just as we were leaving, they said, "Bye now. Goodbye Myna. A Myna bird is what you have. They speak more clearly than a parrot ever could. Your Myna spoke better than any Myna that I have ever heard!"

What a morning this has been. Back to the house and we will have cherries for us and black pitted cherries for Myna bird.

It was a beautiful Saturday afternoon when we took Myna in his cage to our shaded patio and put his cage under a large umbrella. The bird loved the breezes blowing through its feathers. This was also a good time for me to pull the bottom drawer from under his cage. This drawer caught Myna's uneaten food and feces. I dumped it into the rose bed. Then I put the hose sprayer on it until that stainless drawer was clean and put into its slide under Myna's cage. I also cleaned his food trough and his watering cup.

It seemed that Myna bird had an attitude going on about all of this moving of his personal home, so I poured his favorite beverage into his cup (beer). I also dropped a bunch of seedless grapes into his cage. I had a happy bird. Now Jeanette and I decided to have a brew too, along with our Myna bird.

Then who should come around the house to our back patio but three newspapermen. They had heard of this miracle bird. They were on the patio surrounding the cage. They were all around us shooting flash cameras at Myna. Before we could see, Myna had become rigid with fear at those strange machines clicking and flashing bright lights into his eyes.

They said to us, "Make it speak!! Make it speak!!" Myna shut up like a clam—out of fear—out of anger—I don't know. All I know is that the next day the newspaper said, "The bird that we visited was a sham! He did not say a word because birds cannot talk." We read this in the papers the next day. We were getting along with our afternoon rest and we resumed our position on the patio.

We set our large twenty-four-inch fan to blow above our bodies and our patio furniture. Behind that fan we had a hose that threw a light spray behind the fan. This resulted in a very fine cool mist settling over our bodies where we lay prone on blankets and flat patio cots. We loved it and we got a fine tan at the same time without getting burnt up by sunlight. As you know, birds hate to be rained upon, but the Myna bird did not seem to mind feeling this fine mist. We saw Myna bird grooming himself. It was probably an hour or two in napping under the mist that we decided to stop the water and just feel the fan as we sat in our lounge chairs o the shaded patio. We snoozed. We looked up and saw Myna had lowered his head and was actually taking a nap. Jeanette and I said, "Good idea! Let's nap a bit too." It was late afternoon when we awakened. That nap did the trick. We were full of energy. That's when I said, "Let's take Myna out of his cage and let him move around the patio to enjoy his freedom." I felt Myna really loved us. Myna was ready to re-enter his clean cage after a bit of freedom on the patio table. Then he suddenly decided to take flight. It was then I said, "My God! What have I done!" Because Myna flapped his wings several times and lifted into the air and flew away.

Myna's flight was short-lived for he hit that big old oak tree in the back yard and fell to the ground. We knew it must have killed itself on the impact with the tree. I had forgotten we had trimmed his wings so he could not fly. Now our beloved Myna bird was laying on the ground. We bent down and saw he was still breathing.

We put him on a towel and said, "Let's go to the vet right away. It's just down the street. It is a new place just built this year." It's even within walking distance. The dog owners loved it.

I hoped to love it too if they have a veterinarian that can treat our beloved Myna bird. We waited in the lobby holding our Myna in its towel. We wondered could it be just knocked out or dazed or critically injured.

The nurse said, "The vet will see you now." We walked slowly into his examination room and presented our Myna to the vet. He said, "Just lay it right here on the table so I may see what injuries there might be and if it will survive whatever tragedy has befallen him." I said, "Doctor, it is just that Myna flew into a tree." The vet said, "Didn't turn his wings in in time, eh? I said, "No, we didn't trim his wings, but we are new to parenting a Myna bird." He said, "Go to the lobby and wait there while I see to him. I will let you know the results."

The nurse came out an hour later. We were reading a book about Myna birds. She was smiling ear-to-ear and said, "My dear, your Myna is alive and well, except for a broken leg, which we have placed a splint so it may heal. We also trimmed his wings. Bring your Myna back in six months and we will trim them again. It is a delicate thing to trim wings. The doctor might hit bone or a blood vessel. Certainly, don't try it yourself."

The Myna was given back to us in a wee cage. The nurse said, "When you come back bring Myna back in this small cage." We left that vet's office a happy couple and returned home and everyone had a brew–even Myna too!

It was the next afternoon when Joe cam by again and entered and said, "Here's our cooler of beer", and he heard that familiar cry, "Come in! Come in! What do ya know Joe?" I said, "It's a good sound to me my friend." Joe said, "Now wake up Jeanette ad we will have a new brew that I have bought for us to try." Jeanette joined us and sat back in her recliner and enjoyed this cool treat. We gave Myna some too. He would have nothing to do with it. We dumped his drink on a carpet and gave him what he was used to. He wouldn't drink any beer now. Now maybe like real people, he was refined and becoming a tea-totaler. In fact, this is exactly what we gave him—sweet tea!—Lipton tea and he loved it.

There was one more gigantic exciting thing that happened with Myna. Our mean old cat had jumped from the table to the top of Myna's cage with the intent of finding a way to get in there and kill Myna. The cat was shaking the cage and trying to knock it off its stand where it could possibly bust open the door of the cage so the cat could get to Myna.

Suddenly, as quickly as a snake, Myna leaped ad grabbed that nosey cat's nose and bit the cat on the nose. The Myna bird would not let go of the cat's nose and the cat let out a huge yowl that we all could hear. It leaped onto the floor and ran through that screen door like it wasn't there.

We never saw that cat in the neighborhood again. We felt that even after raising it, we did not like that cat. I guess we are just not cat people. I needed to mend the screen door and I re-secured the Myna's cage. We found a portion of the cat's nose in the tray of Myna's cage. I again saw an unusual change in Myna's attitude. I guess it felt secure in knowing it could defend itself.

So, in closing, Myna is happy and we are happy. We still wondered how it would be if my wife and I had a child or children, but that would be another story.

I have made the story clear between bird and cat, but Myna's real name is "Pretty Boy". I originally taught him his name and that he should say,

"I am Pretty Boy", then "Pretty Boy" shortened it to "I Pretty Boy", then he shortened it to "I Pretty" or "I Boy". I think "Pretty Boy" is getting lazy with his bird talk.

There are so many more things I could tell you about Myna bird but this is the time to bring this short story to an end. So bless you until we meet again!

BLACK POODLE
VS
BLACK CAT

BY

WILLIAM L. MILBORN

BLACK POODLE VS BLACK CAT

I have to tell you my last short story is a phenomenon between two creatures—A black poodle named Bart and my black cat. I need you to know that wine or a little drinking seems to help my thinking. So let me tell you about my beloved black Bart and my black cat.

Right from the beginning when Bart was a puppy and cat was a kitten, they nestled in a basket together. It didn't seem too unusual for them to be close. It only became curious to me to see that as they grew, their friendship was more than normal between a cat and a dog. But my little precious ones seemed as happy as they could be. My miniature poodle, black Bart, was no larger in size than my black cat and because of their being equal in size, I think that they thought of each other as not to be a physical challenge or any threat at all.

They were out of the basket now. They had grown beyond puppy and kitten stage. They are now playing. First black Bart crawled close by and chased black cat and after a while black cat would chase black Bart. It was a game that was not played between dogs and cats. Normally it is a game of aggression between cats and dogs, but not in my back yard. Obviously, they were playing. Black Bart was still a puppy and black cat had just matured from a kitten when I noted black cat had climbed upon the back of black Bart and they were romping about the back yard—as a cowboy would on a bronco—except Bart strolled around the yard carrying his playmate black cat.

I think Bart liked the feel of cat's paws grasping and ungrasping his shoulders. I noticed after such play, they would roll to the ground and just lay there for a time. Now hear this, I would put out in a dish both tuna and beef pieces to see what would happen. Amen, they both ate out of the same dish without a snarl or a growl. I thought, here are two pets that somehow have acquired a psychological gift, and I loved it.

I bought a toy full of cat nip for black cat and plain rubber ball for Bart. Even then black cat would let Bart nose his cat nip toy. It cannot be! If ever that could start a war, that would be it. Cat had no interest in Bart's red ball so both played with their toys without complaint. Oh, how they would love to challenge the many neighborhood dogs as they chased across my yard. They were a pair to be reckoned with.

It was only when a land turtle decided to visit that Bart and cat became so totally confused. The cat knocked it around awhile and so did Bart and when that turtle's head popped out of its shell, it would snap its teeth and then Bart and cat decided to let the turtle have its freedom to trespass over their lawn.

It was so nice when I lay back in my reclining chair in the evening and Bart gave leeway to black cat to sit in my lap, where cats are supposed to lay. My little black Bart fit precisely between my hip and the arm of the chair.

I had a hand for each to show my love and scratched both of their backs and behind their ears. We would commonly go to sleep that way. They were soon to awaken for another interesting day.

I forgot to mention that when a delivery man came to our door and knocked or rang the bell, black Bart and black cat stood ready to meet who ever it was that rang the bell and knocked on what they considered their door. When I opened the door, I am now ashamed to say, they both leaped toward the service door in a most unfriendly fashion. The meowed and barked and the cat screeched with a most horrendous sound and Bart barked in his meaningful way. Needless to say that a visitor or a delivery person would leave right away.

In Bart and cat's thinking, they had just won a war. I scolded them but they did not care. I wondered what to do because I was afraid I would get no deliveries or my friends wouldn't come by. What to do?

My poodle, black Bart, and my black cat–what to do? I can't schedule visitors, service or delivery men to come to my door at a time when black Bart and black cat were not in the room. What to do? What to do? An epiphany came to me. Since most service and delivery people would come before noon, I finally settled on an idea that my daughter gave to me. I will put up a barricade in the kitchen where their sleeping baskets are and place it so that they can yowl and yap to their heart's content as I receive friends and service people at my door.

The media had heard that there appeared to be a romance between a dog and a cat. My goodness, did that excite the imagination of the media to do stories about black Bart and black cat.

Now, let me tell you more a out our beautiful poodle named Bartholomew Joshua Briar Patch The Third. In a few months cat and Bart somehow grew apart. The cat was not giving all of his attention to the other cats in the neighborhood. The cat was spending more time flirting with the felines in the neighborhood than playing with Bart or sitting with me.

My best friend Bart, who is my precious, smart little puddle, also a miniature was jealous of the tie and attention I was giving to the cat. Every chance he had Bart was yapping with his quick little barks at the cat. I then decided I needed to distract Bart from the cat and his concern about the cat. So, I wrestled with him on the floor and played hide-n-seek. He loved playing hide-n-seek with me. He loved to ride around on the top of my back like he had bested me or conquered me. Every time I got on my hands and knees to play, he would get on my back and I would try to buck Bart off. I would let him win. No dog ever loved fetch more than Bart did!

I would bounce that little rubber ball all over the place and Bart would chase it like it was a rabbit. Occasionally, the ball would roll into a place where he couldn't reach it no matter how much he pawed for it. Bart would always come running to me to let me know we had a problem about that ball. I would always fetch it for him. When I was tired of playing hide-n-seek, fetch and wrestling, Bart would start throwing the ball into the air and fetch it on his own. There are just a couple more things I would like to tell you about Bart. Bart didn't weigh much more than a seven-pound sack of potatoes. So, when I finally taught him to bring in the newspaper, it was a challenge for he had to bring it up one step onto the porch and then into the house.

Whenever I would give him a treat and pet him, I also would constantly say, Good Boy! Good Boy Bart! He learned to do this trick with some flair except for the Sunday paper. Try as he might he couldn't grasp that paper and walk it to the porch. Even Bart had an epiphany. He grabbed hold of one end of that newspaper and backed to the house dragging that big heavy newspaper. Then he got on the porch, reached down and grabbed its plastic sack and with much effort finally pulled that big heavy paper onto the porch. I opened the door and said, "Good Boy!" I then made Bart bring that big heavy newspaper to my front chair.

Never let it be said that you cannot reach a wonderful communication between your best friend (your dog) and yourself. What does it take? Love–time–and patience and occasionally a treat. The last cute thing I will tell you about Bart is that when I reached for my shoes to go outside to the yard, he beat me to the door and was ready. Besides our regular games, there was one I wish to mention in closing. I had a wonderful big tomato garden. The tomatoes were large and the plants were close together. If I saw one that had fallen off the vine, I had nothing more to do than point to that tomato and Bart would fetch it for me. The tomato was never too large for him not to manage to bring it to me. Commonly it had little teeth marks on the tomato. That was okay.

The cat still required his moments in my lap but beyond that there was no love lost. We have become like some couples I know. They lived together but necessarily love each other. Bart and I, of course, remained bosom buddies and in short, we loved one another.

Though cat and I only have a casual relationship, now he requires that I fulfill the requirements of ownership by allowing me to scratch his back and feed him with regularity.

Printed in the United States
By Bookmasters